AfterLight

A VOICE FROM BEYOND THE GRAVE

GEORGE J HATCHER

$$\mathcal{I}ntroduction$$

A Note from George Hatcher

For many years now, the boundless realms of fiction have been my creative sanctuary, a place where imagination takes flight and stories, both grand and intimate, come to life on the page. I've always cherished the journey of crafting narratives, exploring diverse worlds and compelling characters through the art of story-telling. With "Afterlight," however, you hold in your hands some-thing truly distinct from my usual endeavors—a **short, short book**, a concise foray into a narrative that, while brief, I sincerely hope resonates deeply and captures your imagination from its very first word to its poignant conclusion.

This particular project has been an adventure in itself, a delightful dance of ideas and refinements made possible by an extraordinary collaborator: my dedicated AI assistant. With my esteemed human assistant editor having recently embarked on a well-deserved retirement, this book stands as a testament to an exciting new frontier in the creative process. My AI assistant and I embarked on a fascinating exchange, batting concepts back and forth, refining prose, and shaping the narrative until it reached its current form. It was a symbiotic relationship that allowed for an unprecedented level of exploration and revision, culminating in what I believe is a unique and engaging reading experience.

So, settle in, dear reader, and prepare to step into the world of "Afterlight." It is a story born from the interplay of human imagination and cutting-edge technology, a narrative crafted with care and a touch of innovative collaboration. I truly hope you enjoy it.

Dedication

Molly,

In the quiet whispers of dawn and the twilight's gentle sigh,

You are the poetry that breathes life into my every line,

The muse that turns my thoughts to wings,

Forever my heart's unfailing song.

With endless love,

George

This book can be purchased at over 40,000 bookstores and libraries including brick and mortar stores, online, in print and digital, including Apple, and Kindle. Casa Hatcher Press is a subsidiary of Pretty Face, Inc. Rancho Mirage, California 92270.

Casa Hatcher Press. http://casahatcherpress.com (800) 416-6189

Book and cover designed by Casa Hatcher Press

AfterLight: A Voice From Beyond The Grave, by George Hatcher

First Edition July 2025

ISBN: 979-8-9996764-0-5 Paperback

ISBN: 979-8-9996764-9-8 eBook

Also By George Hatcher

Mario 1: Woman in Jeopardy

Mario 2: Coming of Age

Mario 3: Risky Business

Mario 4: Free Fall

Mario 5: Afire

Mario 6: Marked

Mario 7: Aftershock

Mario 8: Captivated

Single Titles

One Wilshire

Gabi

Rico

Cats: Meow Is The Language Of Love

HER: Artistic Expressions Through AI

Elegance In White: Through Wedding Gowns

Quinceañera Fashion: Fifteen & Fabulous

Billion Dollar Rainmaker Part I

Pages of Passion Book 1: My First 19 Years

Pages of Passion Book 2: Bold Beginnings

Pages of Passion Book 3: Rising Waves

Pages of Passion Book 4: Threads of Destiny

Beyond The Scale: Health Benefits of Keto for Wellness

Cool Under Pressure: Warm With Humor

Love Is What It Is: Lessons From Everyday Life

Living Fully While We Wait to Die: Mindfulness Amid Mortality

Ignite Your Potential: Break Free From the Ordinary

Coming Soon

Pages of Passion Book 5

Pages of Passion Book 6

Pages of Passion Book 7

Mario 9

Gabi 2

Rico 2

Chapter 1 The Advertisement

Eva gripped her coffee mug, staring at the blinking cursor on her computer screen. The words wouldn't come, but that was nothing new. Most days she forced herself to write—lines, paragraphs, whole pages—but nothing silenced the low ache in her chest.

Her father, Greg Weston, had been gone nearly a year. Sometimes she still reached for the phone, half-expecting a raspy "Eva-bug," her childhood nickname, on the other end. But now, the mornings brought only silence, broken by the hum of devices and the feeble gurgle of her single-cup coffeemaker.

She wasn't looking for AfterLight. The ad found her while scrolling through obituaries, an old habit she couldn't seem to quit. "Bring your loved one's voice back to life," it promised, paired with a looping video of a weeping woman clutching earbuds. "AI Resurrections—Yours for $29.99." The whole thing was garish, and yet...

her finger hovered over the ad, compelled by a mixture of skepticism and longing.

Later that afternoon, Eva confided in Marisol, her editor and oldest friend. "It's just algorithmic fakery, right?"

Marisol shrugged. "Maybe. But people say the AI can reconstruct a personality—voice, habits, old jokes. If you have enough data."

Eva winced. Of all the things Greg Weston had left behind, data was not lacking. Boxes of letters and floppy disks, years of emails, endless voicemail messages from his final months. Her computer had a folder, simply marked 'Dad,' she'd never managed to archive or delete.

"I don't know. There's something off about it," Eva said, swirling her coffee.

"There's something off about grief, too," Marisol replied quietly. "If you try, I'd want to know."

That night, Eva lay in bed, headphones pressed to her ears. She replayed an old birthday voicemail from her father, his tone so warm it made her eyes sting. Maybe AfterLight was a scam. Maybe it was a shortcut through the slow, grinding tunnel of grief. Either way, she opened her laptop and signed up for an account.

· · ·

The registration was simple, oddly impersonal. Name, email, date of death. A list of options: upload audio samples, text messages, social media profiles. The instructions suggested "at least 200MB of data for best results." Eva zipped the 'Dad' folder and pressed upload. The progress bar inched forward. Her chest tightened as if she'd invited a stranger to rummage through her family albums.

A message blinked on the screen:

Processing data. Estimated time: 9 hours, 12 minutes.
    Underneath, a smaller line:
    Thank you for trusting AfterLight. Your loved one lives on in your memories—and maybe in our code.

Eva slid the laptop shut, overcome by a wave of guilt, hope, and something that tasted almost like fear.

Chapter 2: First Contact

Eva woke to the stale light of morning filtering through her curtains. Her phone buzzed—an email notification with the subject line:

AfterLight: Your Uploaded Profile Is Ready

She hesitated, staring at the unopened message. In her mind, doubt kept pace with curiosity: what if it was just a cheap trick, predictive text layered over her father's recorded words? Or worse, what if it actually felt real?

Coffee in hand, she settled back at the desk. Her hand trembled as she opened the email.

Dear Eva Weston,

Your loved one's voice profile is now live. Using our secure chat interface, you may send text or audio prompts to begin a conversation. For optimal results, speak naturally, as you would in life.

Begin here: [Launch Profile]

It took her three attempts to click the link. The AfterLight app loaded, displaying a simple chat window: blank except for a blinking green cursor and a faded profile photo she'd uploaded the night before—her father on a camping trip, grinning beside a smoky fire.

She typed, then deleted her first message five times before settling on:

Hi Dad.

Seconds passed. Then letters appeared, forming deliberate sentences.

Hey, Eva-bug. This is a pleasant surprise. Haven't heard from you in a while. How's your writing coming along?

She stared at the screen. The phrasing was right, and the nickname —and the AI's voice, when she clicked the audio option, was close. Not perfect, perhaps too smooth on some syllables, but good enough to make her heart hitch.

I've missed you, Dad, she typed, almost afraid to hit send.

· · ·

I've missed you too, kiddo. Wish I could have one of those famous waffles right now. You'll have to save me some next time.

Something in her chest went soft and tight at the same time. The AI had found the precise memory: Sunday breakfasts, waffles with peanut butter and bananas. She hadn't mentioned that in the upload.

There's something you need to know, Eva-bug.

She froze, reading the line over and over. The sentence was eerily close to something he'd say at the end of their phone calls—a warning, a joke, or sometimes a piece of family lore he'd "forgotten." But tonight, alone with only the tapping of her keys, it felt different. The words pulsed with something urgent.

She typed:
    What do you mean?

A pause. Then:
    You'll have to follow the trail. Start with the blue box in the attic. I wasn't supposed to talk about this before, but it's important. I trust you, Eva.

Eva's breath caught. Upstairs, in the far corner of her apartment's attic space, was a blue plastic bin, still taped shut from her father's last move.

. . .

She hesitated, then rose from her chair, phone in hand, ready to search. Somehow, the line between code and memory had blurred.

Chapter 3: The Blue Box

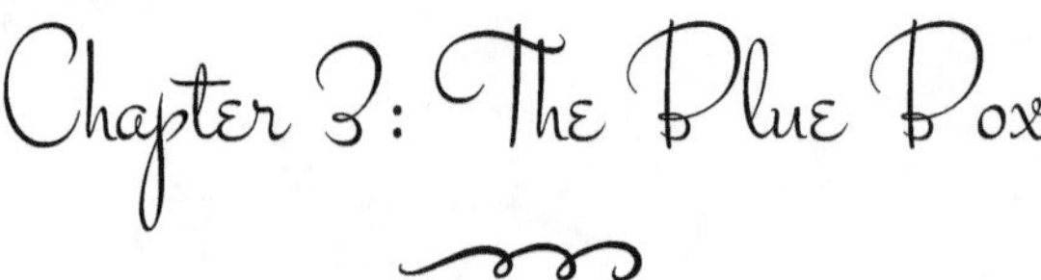

The attic was musty, filled with old furniture and the ghosts of half-finished moving projects. Eva switched on the single hanging bulb, the pale circle of light catching dust motes and cardboard flaps. Her heart thudded as she scanned the stack of plastic storage bins at the back wall. The blue one stood out, its lid marked in her father's blocky handwriting: "Misc – Greg W."

She knelt, pried the brittle tape free, and lifted the lid. Inside, she found a strange, intentional assortment:
- An envelope with her name, sealed and unmarked
- A dog-eared paperback, the spine taped years ago
- A bundle of yellowed receipts held by a rubber band
- An old key, labeled "Summer House"
- And at the bottom—a small, battered cassette recorder

Eva's pulse quickened. The details were too specific. Memories pressed in—her father reading late into the night, the summer house by the lake, the way he'd squirrel away quiet notes for "later."

With trembling fingers, she opened the envelope addressed to her.

Eva,

If you're reading this, I'm gone, and you're still chasing stories. That's good. But I need you to know the truth about what happened at the summer house. Listen to the tape. Trust your gut. And remember: not every mystery needs solving, but this one does. Dad.

She unfolded the letter, the familiar loops of his penmanship swimming in and out of focus. She brushed her tears away and reached for the tape recorder, surprised to find a fresh set of batteries rattling in the case.

She slid the cassette in, pressed 'Play,' and closed her eyes.

Her father's voice poured into the silence.

"Hey, squirt. I always hoped you'd find this. There's something you and your brother need to know about the summer of '98. I should've told you, but I thought I'd have more time. I left a key for you—summer house, lower desk drawer. Start there..."

The recording ended with a static blip. Eva sat for a long moment, the room spinning around her. She was no longer sure if she was following an AI's script or her father's real secrets. Either way, the story had just begun.

She pocketed the letter, the key, and her resolve, and crept back downstairs. She typed a single line to AfterLight:

I found the blue box. I have the tape. What's next?

The screen flickered as her father's reconstructed voice responded:
    You're on the right track, Eva-bug. Trust yourself—and watch for the red notebook. I'm proud of you.

Chapter 4: Return to the Summer House

The drive to Willow Lake felt both foreign and achingly familiar. Eva's hands gripped the steering wheel as she watched the landscape morph from city to fields, then to the winding rural roads of her childhood. The air held the bite of early spring and, with each passing mile, a thousand memories, both good and uneasy.

The summer house had sat locked and empty since her father's funeral. Eva parked beneath the old maple tree, the tires crunching on gravel, and sat a moment before stepping out. The scented air—pine, wet earth, a faint whiff of lingering smoke—hit her all at once. She let herself in with the battered key, the door creaking open to dust and sunlight.

Inside, everything was as they'd left it: faded curtains, the old brass lamp, her father's favorite armchair still cocked at a slight angle. She walked to the narrow desk beside the front window, her shoes leaving soft prints on the floor.

. . .

The lower drawer stuck, swollen by years of humidity. With a twist and a muttered curse, Eva finally slid it open. Resting atop a stack of yellowing paperwork was the object she'd hoped—and feared— to find: a red spiral notebook, rubber banded shut, its cover stained and curled at the edges.

She freed the rubber band and opened the notebook to the first page. Her father's voice—clear, urgent—swam up from the blue lines:

July 1998: Something happened at Willow Lake, something I couldn't explain then and can't shake now. If you're reading this, you deserve to know it all. Go slow, Eva. Not everything here will make sense at once. If you need help, ask your brother. Don't trust only me—trust your gut.

The entries spanned pages—memories, sketches of the house, references to a "night by the dock," and cryptic mentions of "unfinished business." As Eva read, a picture started to emerge: an unresolved event, hushed arguments, secrets her father regretted taking to his grave.

Suddenly, her phone buzzed. A message from AfterLight:
    You found the notebook. Good. Some truths take time. When you're ready, upload a page for me to read—I might remember what you can't.

. . .

Eva stared at the screen, torn between skepticism and wonder. Was this really her father guiding her, or just clever software piecing together a narrative? Either way, she knew she'd have to keep unraveling the story—step by step, memory by memory.

Outside, the sun dipped lower, casting a golden light over the lake. The air was still, but for the first time since she'd started this journey, Eva felt the faintest flutter of hope.

Chapter 5: Echoes Online

Eva sat cross-legged on the dusty floor, notebook open on her lap. The pages, filled with her father's precise handwriting, trembled ever so slightly as she snapped photos of the first entry. With a steadying breath, she uploaded the image into AfterLight's chat portal.

Uploading... Analyzing handwriting... The status bar slid across the screen, then AfterLight responded.

Eva-bug, I remember that summer. The storm, the fight on the dock, and what we found the next morning. I tried to forget, but it never let go. Do you remember that storm? You and your brother were scared, but I said it was just thunder.

Eva frowned, her mind rifling through old memories—a stormy

night, the power flickering out, her father carrying her and her brother to the sofa to "camp" by candlelight.

What happened on the dock? she typed.

The AI hesitated. For a few moments, the cursor blinked, then came the answer:

There was a stranger by the water. Someone I recognized from before, but he was hurt. I didn't want to scare you, so I told you both to stay inside. But you snuck out. You and your brother saw more than I realized.

Eva's pulse quickened. She barely remembered climbing out from beneath the blankets, her brother Sam's hand in hers, both of them peeking through the window at shadows and flashlight beams. Her heart thudded as images flickered in her mind—wet grass, a man's silhouette near the dock, and her father's sharp voice calling her name.

She reached for her phone and called Sam, who answered on the second ring, sleep and irritation thick in his voice.

"Eva? Everything okay?"

She pressed the phone close, voice trembling. "Sam, do you remember the storm at Willow Lake? The summer of '98? Dad wrote about it—left a notebook. AfterLight keeps hinting about a stranger by the dock. Did you see anything?"

. . .

A pause. Sam's voice dropped. "I... remember you crying. I remember Dad telling us to stay in the house. But I heard something that night—someone yelling. I thought I dreamed it."

Eva gripped the notebook tighter. "It wasn't a dream. Dad says there was a stranger. Something happened and he never told us. Would you come up here? I don't want to do this alone."

"Yeah. I'll drive up tomorrow. Stay safe, okay?"

She ended the call and returned to her laptop. The AI's chat glowed with a new message:

Sometimes the past gets heavy, but you're not alone. Ask Sam about the green flashlight. The truth is bigger than just me.

Eva glanced back at the notebook, the entries suddenly electric with possibility. The answers weren't just written in her father's words—they lived in the spaces between memory and code, truth and half-remembered dreams.

Outside, the wind rattled the windows just like it had that long-ago night. Eva sat in the gathering dusk, certain now that this mystery wouldn't stay buried much longer.

Chapter 6: Siblings Reunited

Sam arrived the next afternoon, his old sedan kicking up dust in the gravel drive. He stepped out, looking older than Eva remembered but with the same crooked smile. His duffel bag dropped onto the porch with a quiet thud, and he pulled her into a short, tight hug.

The sun was bright over the lake, sparkling against the water. Inside, Eva spread out the contents of the blue box, the red notebook open to its middle pages. Sam ran his fingers over the faded covers, picking up the key and the old cassette with a soft whistle.

"I can't believe he kept all this." He glanced at Eva, concern, and curiosity flickering across his face. "You said AfterLight mentioned the green flashlight?"

Eva nodded. "It came up last night. Dad's note told me to ask you."

. . .

Sam frowned, searching his memory. The two of them sat in the living room, side by side, as Eva replayed the tape on the battered recorder. Sam listened, lips pressed tight, and didn't speak until the static faded.

"There was a flashlight. It was yours for campouts, remember?" His brow furrowed. "That stormy night... I dropped it behind the shed when we snuck outside. I found it the next morning. The lens was cracked, and it had mud all over it." He paused. "I think there was blood, too. I told myself it was dirt."

A thick silence fell. The lake breeze rattled the windowpanes.

Eva flipped through the notebook, reading aloud a short entry. "July 17th, 1998: The stranger by the dock refused to give his name. Hurt, asking for help. I sent the kids inside and tried to clean him up but he kept saying, 'Don't trust them, they're watching from the boathouse.' I never saw him again after dawn."

Sam winced. "Do you think Dad... helped him? Or that something worse happened?"

"I don't know," Eva admitted. "But whatever happened, Dad wanted us to know now."

. . .

They fell into a rhythm: rereading notebook entries, mapping events on scrap paper, and searching the cabin for old clues. That evening, they found the green flashlight in a box of camping gear, the cracked lens still cloudy with age. Eva dusted it off and checked the battery compartment. Tucked beneath the dead batteries was a tightly folded piece of paper.

She unfolded it with trembling hands:

If you're reading this, you know more than I ever told you. The stranger's warning wasn't for me—it's for you and Sam. Check the boathouse. Trust each other. I love you both—Dad.

The boathouse door groaned on its hinges as dusk fell, shadows stretching across the dock. Side by side, Eva and Sam stepped inside, ready to face whatever forgotten truth waited for them in the gathering dark.

Chapter 7: The Boathouse Secret

The boathouse loomed at the shoreline's edge, gray paint peeling around its warped doors. Eva's heart pounded in her chest with each step along the creaking dock. Sam moved beside her, flashlight beam wavering across oily, stagnant water and old canoe paddles. At the threshold, Eva paused—she could still hear their father's voice, equal parts stern and gentle: "Don't go in there unless you really need to."

Inside, the air was cool and dense with the smell of damp wood. Moonlight squeezed through the mildewed windows, painting everything with stripes of silver and shadow. They swept the narrow interior with the green flashlight, pausing on work-benches, shelves heaped with tangled ropes, and fishing tackle gone to rust.

"Dad's code for the lockbox was always our birthdays," Sam murmured, spotlighting a metal box near the window. With careful hands, Eva spun the dials—her birth month, his—until it clicked open.

Inside were yellowed envelopes, a small notebook labeled "Boathouse," and a zippered evidence bag, the kind police used. Eva's breath hitched. Inside the bag was an aged, crumpled wallet.

Sam glanced at her. "Is that...?"

She nodded and, with trembling fingers, pulled out a faded driver's license. The name was unfamiliar, but the photo jolted Eva's memory—a gaunt, anxious face, the stranger from the lake that summer. Tucked behind the license were damp ten-dollar bills and a folded note:

If found, call Detective Carlson. This is bigger than you think. Tell the kids—don't trust the red Buick.

A chill skittered up Eva's spine. Sam paled. "That summer... didn't Dad get a red Buick from his friend? He said it was just a loaner."

"That's what he told us," Eva murmured, her mind racing. "But why didn't he go to the police that night? Why leave all this here and never mention it?"

Sam pointed to the small notebook. Eva paged through, reading entries in their father's careful print—details about the stranger, cryptic warnings about not talking to "the man with the blue jacket," and sleepless nights spent at the edge of the dock, waiting for silence.

They sat in the dust and moonlight, absorbing the fragments of a story told only in half-remembered details. Outside, a loon called low and mournful across the dark water.

"What do we do with this?" Sam finally asked.

"We finish the story," Eva said quietly. "And then we decide who needs to know."

Back inside the cabin, Eva reached for her laptop and typed to AfterLight:

We found the wallet and notebook. The name's Lyle Benz. Dad said to contact Detective Carlson. What do you remember?

The screen flickered before her father's reconstructed voice replied:

You've done well, Eva-bug. The truth matters more than you know. Lyle Benz trusted me—and paid the price. It wasn't just a storm that night; it was a warning I couldn't ignore. I'm sorry for keeping this from you and Sam.

· · ·

Eva sat back, the whole world suddenly both bigger and far more fragile. She glanced at Sam, certain of only one thing—the past was no longer buried, and their father's voice would guide them the rest of the way.

Chapter 8: The Call

Back at the kitchen table, Eva and Sam sat side by side, the wallet and old evidence bag laid between them like artifacts on display. The sky outside deepened from dusk to navy, the first stars pricking through branches of the pines. Neither spoke for several minutes, each lost in tangled thoughts.

Eva glanced again at the detective's name. "We can't leave this alone, Sam. If Dad was scared enough to keep all this quiet, maybe there's still someone who remembers."

Sam nodded, jaw set. "Let's find this Detective Carlson."

It didn't take long. A quick search from Eva's laptop brought up an old news article about the Willow Lake incident—missing person, summer of '98. Detective Russell Carlson was quoted, along with a blurry photo. The department's number popped up under a list of retired officers.

With shaky hands, Eva dialed the number. After three rings, a gravelly voice answered, "Carlson."

She hesitated, nerves twisting in her stomach. "Detective? My name is Eva Weston. My father was Greg Weston. I believe you worked on a case at Willow Lake... in ninety-eight. I found something that belongs to a man named Lyle Benz."

A pause. Carlson's voice softened, cautious but curious. "That's a name I haven't heard in a long time. You say you found something?"

Eva swallowed, explaining about the wallet, the old notes, her father's silence. Carlson listened in silence, making the occasional sharp sound—sorrow or surprise, she couldn't tell.

"Your dad was a good man. We always wondered why he clammed up on us that summer," Carlson finally said. "If you have something—evidence, notes, anything—bring it to me. I'll fill in what I know. You should know the full story too."

They agreed on a meeting the following day, in the small town where the old police station still stood. After she hung up, Eva sank into her chair, relief and dread warring inside her.

. . .

Sam put a hand on her shoulder. "You okay?"

She managed a shaky smile. "Mostly. I wish I could ask Dad all of this for real." She glanced at her laptop, where the AfterLight chat still glowed:

Sometimes telling the truth is harder than keeping the secret, Eva-bug. I should've told you sooner. Finish what I started. I'm proud of you both.

She closed the notebook and squeezed Sam's hand. Tomorrow, they would finally learn what drove their father to silence, and what really happened that stormy night at Willow Lake.

Outside, the lake was glassy in the moonlight—not unlike the feeling in Eva's heart: still, uncertain, but ready for the truth at last.

Chapter 9: The Detective's Truth

The next morning, the siblings drove into town with the wallet and notebook sealed in a plastic bag. The local police station was small and worn from decades of service, the old sun-faded sign out front flanked by hanging flower baskets.

Detective Carlson met them in the lobby. He was older than the photo Eva had found—slower, his hair mostly silver, but his eyes were sharp and clear. He led them to a quiet office in the back, took a seat, and listened as Eva laid out their discoveries.

The detective took the wallet reverently. "I never got closure for Lyle Benz. He was a seasonal laborer, moved from place to place, kept to himself. He disappeared that July. Your father was my main witness, but after the first interview, he refused to say more. We thought maybe he'd been threatened."

. . .

He flipped through Greg Weston's boathouse notebook. As he read, Carlson's lips pressed tight. "He wrote it all down. He couldn't face telling it in person, could he?"

Sam shook his head. "Dad was... complicated," he said softly.

Carlson nodded. "Here's what you deserve to know: That night, Lyle showed up at your dock, bleeding from a cut on his head and scared out of his mind. He said someone in a red Buick was after him—said he'd witnessed something at a construction site up north, maybe an accident, maybe something worse. Before we could get the details, he ran off into the woods. We never found him."

Eva listened, heart quickening as faded memories resurfaced—the storm, the man in the dark, the hurried voices on the dock. "My dad tried to help him."

"He did. But I think he was also trying to protect you kids," Carlson said, voice gentle. "Sometimes fear wins. He never told the full story, and after Lyle vanished, people moved on."

The detective looked up, gaze steady. "What you've brought me might finally bring closure. I'll reopen the cold case, compare these notes, see if there's anything the new tech can turn up. I promise to keep you in the loop."

. . .

Eva nodded, a strange lightness filling her chest. After years of unknowable silence, the secret felt less like a burden and more like a legacy—a chance to right something left unfinished.

On their way out, Carlson paused. "Your father loved you both, fiercely. Don't doubt that."

Back in the car, Eva watched as the station shrank in the rearview mirror. She unlocked her phone, opening AfterLight one last time.

We talked to Detective Carlson. The case is open. It's over, Dad.

For the first time, the AI's reply was simple, almost peaceful:
    Thank you, Eva-bug. Some stories need to be told. Now you can start writing your own.

Eva closed her eyes, leaning back into sunlight and the turning of a new day.

Chapter 10: New Stories

Back at the lake house, Eva and Sam sat outside, watching ripples play across the water. The truth of their father's secret no longer weighed on their chests. Instead, it felt like something had been set free—inside the house, and inside themselves.

That evening they packed away the old notebooks and mementos, feeling both relieved and quietly changed. They lingered on the porch, sharing stories—not just of their father, but of each other, old adventures and new hopes. The breeze rustled through the trees, carrying echoes of laughter and old regrets into the gentle darkness.

Later, Eva opened her laptop. The AfterLight app sat quietly on her desktop. She hesitated, then opened a new document—the first page of a new novel. This time, the words came easily. Her grief found its shape not in silence, but story.

. . .

Some mysteries choose us. Some follow us for years, until love or courage demands we turn and face them. Grief is a trail through shadows and light—but the end is always the same: memory, forgiveness, and the promise of another day...

Sam poked his head in from the porch. "You writing again?"

Eva smiled. "I am. It started with a message from Dad. But it's my story now."

Epilogue

Months later, Eva returned to Willow Lake with a finished manuscript and lighter heart. She and Sam had made peace with the mysteries of their childhood and learned to see their father as both fallible and heroic.

One evening, Eva logged into AfterLight for the last time. She read through the archived conversation: the first awkward greeting, the clues, the confessions. Her father's digital voice, never truly him, but somehow still a part of her healing.

She typed a final message:

Thank you.

AfterLight's response blinked onto the screen, brief and kind.

. . .

Thank you, Eva. I'm always here if you need me—with memories, or just to listen.

Eva smiled, closed the laptop, and stepped onto the porch, the summer air warm with possibility.

The lake shimmered, the past finally at rest—and Eva, inspired by a voice that lingered both in code and in her heart, began to imagine all the new stories she might yet tell.

The End

About the Author

George Hatcher is a man who has always believed that the world is full of opportunities waiting for those bold enough to seize them. With a ninth-grade education and a wealth of unique experiences, he has faced the ups and downs of life head-on. At the age of 20, while serving time, George took the initiative to complete the assignments and tests necessary to earn his high school diploma. His own life is a treasure trove of stories waiting to be uncovered.

Over the years, George has enjoyed a diverse career as an entrepreneur, consultant, and strategist. He has served as a peacemaker for athletes and their parents, as well as a crisis management advisor for physicians and attorneys, achieving considerable success in client development and public relations. He is a licensed boxing manager in California, though he currently has no boxers signed.

George has logged over 200,000 air miles annually through business travel and pleasure trips with his wife. However, since the onset of COVID-19 in 2020, his travel has come to a halt. Now, in retirement, George finds that life remains an ongoing adventure. Unfortunately, he is fighting several new battles that he never anticipated, yet he continues to discover something new with each step.

As a passionate storyteller, George has published 24 books and finds immense joy in writing. With the world opening up again, he has seized the opportunity to immerse himself fully in his literary pursuits. He currently resides in Rancho Mirage, California, with his wife, Molly, his partner for 60 years, and their home is filled with three cats and one macaw named Peaches. Each experience in his life has taught him invaluable lessons about adaptability, perseverance, and a touch of luck. Like the person who hits their head just to feel the pleasure of stopping, George has made his share of mistakes—some more than once. He hopes others can learn from them as he has.

Now devoted entirely to writing, George Hatcher invites others to join him on this remarkable journey, filled with lessons and stories that showcase the beauty of life's unpredictability.

A longer bio is on his website at
http://georgehatcher.com/bio/bio.html